# DOCTOR WHO

**BBC CHILDREN'S BOOKS**
UK | USA | Canada | Ireland | Australia
India | New Zealand | South Africa

BBC Children's Books are published by Puffin Books,
part of the Penguin Random House group of
companies whose addresses can be found at
global.penguinrandomhouse.com.

www.penguin.co.uk
www.puffin.co.uk
www.ladybird.co.uk

Penguin
Random House
UK

**First published 2022**
**001**

**Written and designed by Paul Lang**
**Story Illustrated by Ryan Quickfall**

**Printed in Italy.**

The authorized representative in the EEA is
Penguin Random House Ireland, Morrison Chambers,
32 Nassau Street, Dublin D02 YH68

A CIP catalogue record for this book
is available from the British Library

**ISBN: 978-1-405-95229-3**

All correspondence to:
BBC Children's Books
Penguin Random House Children's
One Embassy Gardens,
8 Viaduct Gardens
London SW11 7BW

# CONTENTS

## FLUX FIXERS

The Flux has jumbled up words from the Doctor's past and scattered them through this book. Help her unlock her memories by solving the anagrams . . .

> I couldn't be the Doctor if I didn't have my TARDIS and my best mates to help me out - so here's everything you need to know about my wonderful blue box and its crew . . .

BOX

POLIC

# MEET THE CREW

## THE DOCTOR

**Oh! That's me! Hello!**

Now, I know what you're thinking. Yes, 'Doctor' is usually a title, not a name, but I think it suits me very nicely. Being the Doctor is like having every job in the universe all at once, and not getting paid for any of them. But I don't mind! Why would I want money anyway? Coins would ruin the line of my coat.

I take being the Doctor very seriously, and I'll always do my best to help anyone in trouble - or just in need of a big hug! Why me? Well, someone's got to help, so why *not* me? I can travel anywhere in space and time, so it would be rude not to.

You'd think that I'd be the most popular person in the galaxy – what with me being so brilliant – but, sadly, life just isn't like that. There are creatures out there who want to do terrible things, and they get annoyed when I try to stop them. Oops!

I've lived for a very long time and haven't always looked like I do now. Although I'm quite attached to this face, so it would be a big shame if I had to change it any time soon.

# THE TARDIS

You're probably wondering how I do the whole 'travelling through space and time' bit. That's where the TARDIS comes in – my time machine! The letters stand for Time and Relative Dimension in Space, because the inside and outside are in different dimensions.

If you saw my TARDIS on the street, you'd think it was an ordinary police box – a special blue phone box once used by officers to summon help, before they had radios or mobile phones. But open those doors and you're in for a big surprise. Remember what I was saying about different dimensions? (Course you do, it was only in the last paragraph.) Well, it means the inside of the TARDIS is bigger than the outside. Just as well, or I wouldn't have anywhere to put all my stuff.

The TARDIS was feeling a bit poorly after it encountered the Flux – an extremely destructive force designed to consume everything in its path. Even the TARDIS couldn't survive it, and I had to do an emergency reset – but we'll come to that later . . .

# THE CREW

**If you have a time machine that's bigger on the inside, you're going to want a few people in there with you, so you don't get lonely. Luckily for me, I travel with the best crew anyone could wish for.**

## YAZ

First up there's my wingwoman, my BFF – the incredible **Yasmin Khan**. Or Yaz to her mates. She's been travelling with me longer than almost anybody else, and I don't know what I'd do without her. Yaz is the kind of woman who spends four years travelling the world to do you a favour, putting herself in terrible danger along the way and generally being the absolute greatest. She was a trainee police officer when we first met, so has loads of skills that have come in very handy on our travels!

## DAN

My newest pal, **Dan Lewis**, joined my gang after he had a Halloween to remember: first, he was kidnapped by a giant dog and taken to an alien spaceship; then his house was miniaturised; and then he helped defeat a Sontaran battle fleet! After that I knew he could handle anything – even me! Dan's a people person, and he's always thinking of others before himself. He also has an annoying habit of working out how his friends feel about stuff before they even know themselves.

**So, that's me, that's the ship, that's the crew – I think that's enough catching up, don't you?**
***Let's get on with some adventures!***

# The (Almost) COMPLETE HISTORY of the Doctor

Having trouble keeping track of my escapades? I don't blame you. Even I struggle occasionally, and I was there - sometimes twice! Here's my timeline so far . . .

## PART 1

### THE GREAT ESCAPE

It all began on Gallifrey, home of the mighty Time Lords. Really dull place: everyone talked dead posh, wore big collars and moaned on about how we mustn't interfere with what was happening on other planets, or in other times. So, I decided to leg it by nicking a TARDIS that was due for repair and heading out into the universe. Danger and adventure, here I come!

### THE TIMELESS CHILD

OK, that's how I always thought my story started. But I keep finding out bits of another story, and people keep telling me that's mine too. In this version, a traveller from Gallifrey called Tecteun was the one who got itchy feet, and decided to explore the universe. But Tecteun found something she wasn't expecting on her travels – a young girl, abandoned and alone, in a far corner of a distant galaxy.

FIRST CONTACT TECTEUN

### UNIVERSE TWO

Tecteun discovered this Timeless Child beneath a wormhole connecting two different universes and decided that the child must have passed through from what she named Universe Two. Pretty big conclusion to jump to, if you ask me! She adopted the foundling and returned to Gallifrey.

### REGENERATION!

Back home, Tecteun became obsessed with studying her new child for clues about where she'd come from, but never found any. Then, disaster! The child had a terrible fall and died. But, amazingly, she began to glow with a ferocious energy that renewed every cell in her body, leaving her with a new face - she'd regenerated.

## LIFE ON EARTH

This Fugitive Doctor settled on Earth disguised as a human called Ruth Clayton, with her original memories safely stored in a biodata module. It was all going fine for her, until a squadron of Judoon hired by Division tracked her down. Reunited with her memories, the Fugitive escaped the Judoon – but they locked me up in her place. Rude!

TURN TO PAGE 16

## FLUX FIXER

**Unjumble the word mixed up by the Flux . . .**

### AGE FRILLY

**CLUE:** a planet from my past – and future!

Answer on page 61

## THE FUGITIVE

Now, this might get confusing, cos the next bit happens to me later, but also has to happen here first. Just roll with it! The grown-up formerly known as the Timeless Child ended up leading a Division team, but struggled with the things her bosses were asking her to do. So, she decided to steal a TARDIS and escape. Familiar, right? Because – you've guessed it – the Timeless Child was me.

## POWER

This only fuelled Tecteun's dedication. There were many more experiments that caused the child to have several regenerations before Tecteun finally worked out the secret of the magical process. She stole it for herself and the people of Gallifrey. With these incredible new powers, they became the Time Lords.

FIRST CONTACT LUPARI

## DIVISION

Remember what I said about how Time Lords didn't like to interfere? Well, that wasn't strictly true. There was a group called the Division, whose sole aim was to guide the course of events across the universe. Tecteun and the Timeless Child were signed up to its ranks. Eventually, Division outgrew Gallifrey, and set up shop in the space between this universe and Universe Two – with Tecteun in charge.

9

When Dan, the Doctor and I got trapped in a self-storage facility with some very angry Daleks, time was not on our side . . .

# DALEK TIME TWISTERS

**1** The Doctor had managed to un-Flux the Flux, but it had damaged the TARDIS. The TARDIS needed a reboot, so we planned a tropical holiday while it healed. But why had we ended up in a Manchester warehouse on New Year's Eve? And what were those nasty-looking cracks on the TARDIS?

**2** Turned out we weren't the only ones seeing in 2022 at ELF Storage. Its owner, Sarah, was there, plus a customer called Nick who had a massive crush on Sarah but was too scared to tell her. Imagine that!

**3** Did I mention the Executioner Dalek? It certainly hadn't come for a quick chorus of 'Auld Lang Syne'. First, it exterminated poor Sarah and Nick. After that, it came for us, furious that the Doctor's actions with the Flux meant the Dalek battle fleet had been blown to smithereens.

**4** Then something very unusual happened. The Dalek *actually* exterminated us! It doesn't usually get that serious with the Doctor around. So how come I'm here to tell you this story? That's where the fun really starts . . .

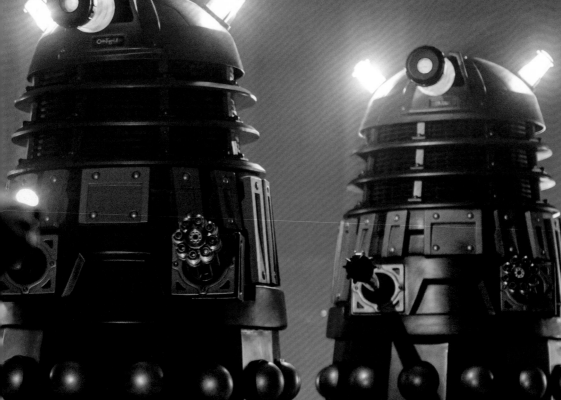

**This wasn't the first time the Daleks had used time to their advantage . . .**

A bunch of devious Daleks from the far future built a time machine to travel back and invade Earth!

Daleks also experimented with time-corridor tech as part of a plan to capture Gallifrey.

**5** We all found ourselves right back where we came in. But so did the Dalek. We were in a time loop, triggered by the TARDIS trying to protect us! As we could remember what had happened last time, maybe we'd survive if we tried something different?

**6** Fat chance! The Dalek got us again. And we soon found there was no escape from the building – it was sealed off with a force field. All we could do was keep going round and hope for a better outcome. Of course, there were complications – for starters, the time loop got shorter by one minute each time. And more Daleks kept appearing, learning from their mistakes too and getting even sneakier.

**7** How did we get out of that one? We realised the Daleks were able to anticipate what we'd learn. So, we staged a 'fake' loop. Instead of simply improving our plan, we did something completely different. That meant we finally had a chance to sneak out, then used a load of hazardous material and fireworks that we'd found in the storage units to create a very big bang. Happy New Year!

Sneaky Dalek Caan loved an emergency temporal shift to get out of a tight spot!

This Dalek turned to stone when it ended up on the wrong side of a crack in time.

11

# FIND THE FRIENDS

Big problem. There's a Dalek execution squad on the loose and I've had to hide my gang's names in this grid to protect them. But there's also a time loop, so they've all ended up in there more than once. Can you find all the names and add up how many times each one appears before the Daleks exterminate us? *You have nine minutes - go!*

Answer on page 61

I FOUND
**YAZ**
◯ TIMES

I FOUND
**DAN**
◯ TIMES

I FOUND
**SARAH**
◯ TIMES

I FOUND
**NICK**
◯ TIMES

# The Doctor's
# FAMILY ALBUM
## PART 1

I don't allow just anyone on board the TARDIS. It takes a very special kind of person to join my crew, and I've been lucky enough to meet loads of people like that on my travels. Some have stayed with me for years, while others came and went in a flash, but I've never forgotten any of them – they're all family to me.

## SUSAN FOREMAN

You're not going to believe this, but Susan is my grandaughter! I know – I don't look old enough, right? But that's not all – for quite a lot of my life I was her grandFATHER. And I might be a grandfather again one day. It's hard to know, being me. Susan tagged along when I made a swift exit from Gallifrey in a stolen TARDIS. She was only a teenager at the time, so I thought it would be a good idea to stay on Earth and send her to school there. I ended up liking the place quite a bit, and the rest is history. After some travelling around, we returned to Earth – in the future, when it lay in ruins after a failed Dalek invasion. Susan decided to stay and help the people rebuild their shattered planet. That's my girl!

## BARBARA WRIGHT and IAN CHESTERTON

Sending Susan to school seemed like a good idea – until two of her teachers, Ian and Barbara, came to the TARDIS one night. Back then, I wasn't quite as friendly as the Doctor you now know and love, so I kidnapped them. After this shaky (and slightly terrifying) start, we all became bezzies, until it was time for them to go home. So, I dropped them back in 1965.

## MELANIE BUSH

Mel and I had a slightly topsy-turvy relationship with time. I was already travelling with her before we met for the first time! Not quite sure how that worked, even now. She was a big fan of carrot juice, while I still can't touch the stuff.

## GRAHAM O'BRIEN and RYAN SINCLAIR

This face's first fam. After seeing what the universe had to offer, this grandad-and-grandson duo went home to Earth so they could use everything they'd learned to make a better world. What could be more perfect?

## LIZ SHAW

Brainy Liz had about ten different degrees and was one of the smartest people I've ever met.

## TURLOUGH

This one was secretly trying to kill me! But we soon sorted that out. Dressed like a schoolboy; actually an alien prince.

13

## THE FLUX

**WHAT IS IT?** A universe-destroying wave of energy designed to wipe out everything in its path.

**WHO CREATED IT?** Tecteun, the Gallifreyan who found me as a child. She feared the influence I was having on the universe, so wanted to wipe everything out and start again – without me!

**HOW DID IT WORK?** By disrupting every particle in the universe, causing the entire structure of the universe to fail.

**HOW DID I STOP IT?** First, I rammed it with the TARDIS, hoping a burst of vortex energy would stop the Flux in its tracks. But, when a second wave was unleashed, I put a Passenger form – a living storage unit – in its path. The Flux is now stored neatly away.

**WHAT HAPPENED NEXT?** The Flux was extinguished, but the damage it did was extensive. And the Daleks weren't very happy at all about their fleet being wiped out.

**Not all weapons are great big guns! These are some of the sneakiest – but most destructive – I've faced . . .**

# SUPER

## THE REALITY BOMB

**WHAT IS IT?** A ferociously powerful weapon designed to obliterate every non-Dalek thing that ever existed, across every possible universe!

**WHO CREATED IT?** Davros, creator of the Daleks. I really wish he would just stop creating things.

**HOW DID IT WORK?** It used waves of Z-Neutrino energy to cancel out the electrical field that holds every atom together. Without that field, everything would become dust, and then even the dust would become nothing. Only Daleks left.

**HOW DID I STOP IT?** I set up an internalised synchronous back-feed reversal loop to close all the Z-Neutrino relay loops, which prevented the bomb from detonating. Then I destroyed it in a (fairly) controlled explosion.

**WHAT HAPPENED NEXT?** Davros and the Daleks were defeated, although some of the barriers between dimensions had been weakened.

## THE MOMENT

**WHAT IS IT?** The most dangerous weapon ever created. It got its name because it could destroy absolutely anything in a single moment.

**WHO CREATED IT?** The Ancients of Gallifrey.

**HOW DID IT WORK?** By creating time fissures – tears in the fabric of reality.

**HOW DID I STOP IT?** I didn't – I used it! At the height of the Last Great Time War between the Time Lords and the Daleks, I wiped them all out in one very big bang. Or did I?

**WHAT HAPPENED NEXT?** Turns out, it didn't happen quite like that at all. The Moment took the form of my old friend Rose Tyler and brought together three different versions of me. Three heads were better than one, and we came up with a much cooler plan (that totally saved Gallifrey).

# WEAPONS

## THE DEATH PARTICLE

**WHAT IS IT?** A Cyberman weapon that could destroy all organic life in the universe.

**WHO CREATED IT?** Ashad, a human who was only part way through being converted into a Cyberman.

**HOW DID IT WORK?** It was a good old-fashioned bomb, so it really would have just blown everything up (well, everything organic, anyway). Ashad's Cybermen – being completely robotic – would have been the only survivors.

**HOW DID I STOP IT?** The Master helped me out a bit by shrinking it down to a fraction of its original size, so its range was limited to just one planet. A man called Ko Sharmus sacrificed his own life to detonate it while the rest of my friends escaped to safety.

**WHAT HAPPENED NEXT?** All remaining life on Gallifrey, home of the Time Lords, perished – although the planet itself is still there.

# The (Almost) COMPLETE HISTORY of the Doctor

You've read all the stuff that was wiped from my memory, so now you know as much about that part of my life as I do. But what about all the adventures I *can* remember?

## PART 2

### THE GREAT ESCAPE

My story begins on my home planet: Gallifrey, home of the Time Lords. But we already did that part – blah, blah, blah, stole a TARDIS, legged it, see ya later! When I left, I looked a bit different from how you know me now. I was a man, for a start! And even though I'm technically much older now, I looked ancient then.

### AN UNEARTHLY CHILD

I wasn't alone – my grandaughter, Susan, had come with me. We settled in East London in the twentieth century. Being an alien, she was a bit stranger than your average kid from 1963, so two of her teachers made an unannounced home visit to see what her story was. And I took them on an unannounced visit to the Stone Age.

### THE DALEKS

I had my first crew – me and Susan, plus teachers Ian and Barbara – travelling together in the TARDIS. After our trip into Earth's past, it was time to go further afield. First stop, Skaro – planet of the Daleks! It was clearly destiny, as the Daleks ended up becoming my biggest enemy.

FIRST CONTACT DALEKS

### SO LONG, SUSAN

The first big change came after we foiled the first Dalek invasion of Earth. Susan had fallen in love with a resistance fighter. I knew she'd never abandon me, but I wanted her to have a chance at a normal life, so I locked the TARDIS doors and told her it was time to leave home.

## FLUX FIXER

**Unjumble the word mixed up by the Flux . . .**

ARGON TEENIER

**CLUE:** a big change for me!

Answer on page 61

## FACING MY PAST

Turns out, you can't just steal a TARDIS and go on the run without consequences, and the Time Lords hauled me up on trial. Obviously, I was guilty as charged, so they basically grounded me. I was confined to the naughty step on Earth, and to make sure nobody I'd met before recognised me, they gave me a new face. Luckily it was a very elegant one! Everything was changing again . . .

**FIRST CONTACT SEA DEVILS**

## IN EXILE

I settled down to my new life, working as chief scientific advisor to UNIT. Everything went swimmingly until my childhood pal the Master turned up looking for trouble. He was almost as charming, witty and handsome as me, but his plans tended to come unstuck because he picked hopeless allies. We lived parallel lives on Earth for a bit. Me on the side of good, and him – evil.

TURN TO PAGE 24

**FIRST CONTACT ICE WARRIORS**

## MONSTER FUN

The adventures kept on coming – me and my pals Jamie and Zoe met a real rogues' gallery of monsters. I also bumped into UNIT – a top-secret army division set up to combat alien invasions of Earth. UNIT's boss, Brigadier Lethbridge-Stuart, became a dear friend.

## END OF THE ROAD

Ian and Barbara eventually left too, but the journey continued alongside a load of new friends. I still ran into the Daleks more often than I would have liked, but it was my first encounter with the Cybermen that led to my next big life event – regeneration!

**FIRST CONTACT CYBERMEN**

## ANOTHER ME!

New face, same old Doctor! Some things about me had changed, of course. I was physically younger, so I could do a lot more mucking around. I liked a laugh – but woe betide anyone who didn't take me seriously, cos I could switch to being scary in a flash.

# THE FLUX
# FRIENDS

I'm not the only new mate the Doctor made while she was sorting out that Flux business. Check out this brilliant bunch . . .

## KARVANISTA

Oh, do we have to start with this bad-tempered hound? They say a dog is a man's best friend, but you could have fooled me after meeting this one. The very first thing he did when we met was kidnap me and take me off to his spaceship! Fair play to the old fleabag though – he did explain it was for my own good.

He was a Lupari, see, and his species had one big job to do – protect humanity. Every Lupari has an assigned human, and it's their duty to make sure no harm comes to them. Lucky me then, because I got Karvanista, who didn't like me one bit. And the feeling was mutual, let me tell you.

## VINDER

Inston-Vee Vinder was one of the first to clap eyes on the Flux. He spotted it approaching from Observation Outpost Rose and tried to let people know, but it was too late. He'd once been the lackey of a nasty fella called the Grand Serpent, but he'd made himself unpopular when he revealed the evil stuff his boss was up to.

Lots of people were frantically looking for loved ones while the Flux was wreaking havoc, including Vinder. His missus, Bel, was missing, and he went to great lengths to track her down.

## JOSEPH WILLIAMSON

This fella had a lot in common with me – he was a Scouser, and a bit of a legend too. Joseph lived in Liverpool about 200 years ago, and was known as the Mad Mole of Edge Hill. He built tunnels under the city, and nobody was ever sure why. It took the Flux coming along to make it all clearer to me.

Poor old Joe must have thought he was going crackers after he did a bit of digging and discovered doors to other universes right under his land. He then built doorways over them, which started shifting around, leaving him even more confused!

## FLUX FIXER
**Unjumble the words mixed up by the Flux . . .**

### INCA WARMER

**CLUE:** a terrible conflict on the border of Eastern Europe.

*Answer on page 61*

## MARY SEACOLE

When the Doctor found herself transported to 1855, she was lucky enough to meet marvellous Mary, a nurse born in Jamaica, who was by then working on the battlefield of the Crimean War.

But the Brits were fighting Sontarans, not Russians (who they were supposed to be fighting, it being the Crimean War and all). And Mary didn't so much as bat an eyelid at the sight of a bunch of alien potatoes getting involved in a load of argy-bargy. The Sontarans were no match for the dream team of Mary and the Doctor though, and were soon in retreat.

## BEL

Poor Bel was having troubles of her own. Her home planet had been destroyed, and she was left dodging Daleks and Cybermen to stay alive. She was pregnant as well, just to make things extra stressy.

Eventually she found a stray Lupari ship and set off to find Vinder. Karvanista wasn't best pleased when he spotted this rogue vessel, so he forced it to join the Lupari shield protecting Earth from the Flux. Our canine companion soon found out how handy Bel was in a fight. Eventually she and Vinder were safely reunited and could finally look forward to their little 'un's arrival.

## PROF. JERICHO

They say you never really know someone until you've spent three years travelling the world with them, trying to prevent a universe-ending disaster. So that means me and Yaz know Eustacius Jericho very well indeed.

He first popped up in 1967, doing research on a woman called Claire, who was plagued by visions of the future. These were linked to the Weeping Angels, who zapped Jericho back to 1901, which is where we came in. The poor fella didn't make it in the end – the Flux got him, and he went on his 'awfully big adventure'.

# Dan's GRAND TOUR

All right folks, it's your favourite Scouse part-time tour guide here. Now, when I'm not saving the universe and that, there's nothing I like better than showing people around places and telling a few tales. See if you can match up my descriptions of some places I've been to with the pictures at the bottom. And, just cos I don't like to make things too easy for you, there's one picture that doesn't have a pair.

**1** Nice spot for a bit of climbing if you're into that sort of thing. Ideal if you want a break from the stresses of everyday life, as there's nobody for miles around. There's a lot of wisdom to be found there, if you know where to look.

MY ANSWER

**2** If you're thinking about making time to drop in here, take my advice and skip it! It's a total tourist trap. And there's every chance you'll get caught up in a time storm and end up seeing things you'll wish you hadn't.

MY ANSWER

**3** I first went to this place when I had to leave a very important message on a wall for a friend – something that could be seen from space. In one timeline, it had a different name after it was conquered by alien invaders.

MY ANSWER

**4** Quite small, this gaff. In fact, blink and you'll miss it. It's the sort of place where strange things happen. Some people say it might be cursed. At one time, it was a top-secret base for a top-secret organisation.

MY ANSWER

**5** Normally I wouldn't go near this city, for personal reasons like, so it really wasn't where I was expecting to end up. Fortunately I didn't spend much time there. I was quite glad to be honest – I found it a bit repetitive.

MY ANSWER

**A** CHINA

**B** MANCHESTER

**C** LIVERPOOL

**D** MEDDERTON

**E** ATROPOS

**F** NEPAL

Answers on page 61

# The Doctor's FAMILY ALBUM PART 2

## JAMIE McCRIMMON
Jings! It's one of my all-time best McMates. It was a culture shock for this young eighteenth-century highlander to be whisked off in the TARDIS, but he took to it like a haggis to water. You wouldn't believe the monsters we saw off: Daleks, Cybermen, Ice Warriors and even the Abominable Snowman. Our fun ended when he was sent home by the Time Lords, with his memories of me completely wiped. That was one of the saddest days of all my lives.

## ROSE TYLER
Rose and I crossed paths just when we needed each other most. I was the last survivor of a terrible war, and her life was just chugging along, ordinary and boring. When we got together, the whole of space and time suddenly seemed like a happier place! I showed her everything and everywhere. For me, it was like seeing it all again for the first time. The Doctor, rebooted! But, just like with all my other friends, our partnership wasn't destined to last. She ended up stranded in a parallel world, all to keep this one safe from Daleks and Cybermen.

## JO GRANT
The 1970s were a weird time for me. I had a job! With a boss! Jo was my lab assistant. Never mind that she didn't have a qualification to her name – Jo was brave and brilliant, and that counted just as much. Everyone loved her, especially me.

## MARTHA JONES
When medical student Martha came along, I was too busy moping about losing Rose to even notice how incredible she was. And she really was! She helped me save Earth more than once.

## BEN & POLLY
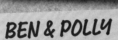

A gorgeous pair who had their first date crashed by me turning up to fight a load of War Machines!

## LEELA

Don't turn your back on this brilliantly feisty warrior – unless you want a poisoned jungle thorn in it. I'm a Time Lord. . . Get Me Out of Here!

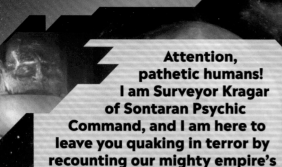

Attention, pathetic humans! I am Surveyor Kragar of Sontaran Psychic Command, and I am here to leave you quaking in terror by recounting our mighty empire's greatest victories against the weak and feeble Doctor!

# THE MOST GLORIOUS TRIUMPHS OF THE SONTARAN EMPIRE

## THE TOTAL VANQUISHING OF EARTH (STAGE 1)

**COMMANDING OFFICER:** Commander Ritskaw
**BATTLE PLAN:** Take advantage of the coming of the Flux to vanquish any surviving species while they were incapacitated. Included a full attack on Earth and the establishment of a base in Liverpool, Great Britain. From there, we would target points in Earth's history as far back as the dawn of time, erasing all traces of humanity.

**OUTCOME: Success!** Ritskaw was killed by a feral Lupari and his command ship was destroyed in the glorious firestorm that followed. But this was all a clever set-up for The Next Total Vanquishing of Earth (Stage 2 of The Total Vanquishing of Earth).

## THE NOT-AT-ALL-DUPLICITOUS INVASION OF TIME

**COMMANDING OFFICER:** Commander Stor
**BATTLE PLAN:** Trick the Time Lords into opening the force field around Gallifrey by staging a fake Vardan invasion, which would be followed by a genuine Sontaran invasion, culminating in the capture of both the planet and the secrets of time travel. The foolish Doctor was tricked into aiding our plan.
**OUTCOME: Success!** Stor and his troops were wiped out when the Doctor used a forbidden weapon called a De-mat Gun. But this also obliterated the event from time and space, so technically the defeat never actually occurred.

## THE MIGHTY SONTARAN CLONE WORLD STRATAGEM

**COMMANDING OFFICER:** General Staal the Undefeated
**BATTLE PLAN:** To conquer the miserable planet Earth and turn its fetid lands over to an honourable new purpose – a vast Sontaran cloning farm. All life on Earth was to be choked to death with poisonous gas. Additional positive outcome: destruction of the Doctor.
**OUTCOME:** *Success!*
The clone world was not established, the Doctor was not destroyed, General Staal the Undefeated was defeated and all other Sontarans died in glorious battle. But it was clear that humans had already made excellent progress in poisoning the air of their world long before our arrival. This intelligence will be useful in future endeavours.

## FLUX FIXER

Unjumble the word mixed up by the Flux . . .

### ORLOP VILE

**CLUE:** location of the Sontaran base on Earth.

Answer on page 61

## THE TOTAL VANQUISHING OF EARTH (STAGE 2)

**COMMANDING OFFICER:** Commander Stenck
**BATTLE PLAN:** Following the complete success of Stage 1, we quickly moved on to Stage 2 – an alliance with the Grand Serpent, who infiltrated the wretched Earth forces of UNIT to disable all defences and allow our invasion forces to reclaim the planet.
**OUTCOME:** *Success!* The entire Sontaran fleet was consumed by the Flux after some typically treacherous actions by the Doctor. But the Cyber and Dalek fleets were also destroyed after receiving false transmissions offering an alliance. *Sontar-HA!*

## THE SCHEME TO DEFEAT THE WRETCHED RUTAN HOST

**COMMANDING OFFICER:** Group Marshal Stike
**BATTLE PLAN:** The Sontaran Empire has been at war with the Rutan Host for as long as anyone can remember, for reasons that are now inconsequential because they have been forgotten by both sides. A plan was devised to steal a crude time vessel, and the Doctor was seized to assist. The plan did not anticipate the arrival of a second Doctor, or the unbearably hot temperatures in the Earth region of Spain.
**OUTCOME:** *Success!* While Group Marshal Stike was stabbed, burned with acid, disintegrated and finally blown up along with his ship, his subordinate Major Varl made the important discovery of an Earth substance known as 'chocolate'.

# The (Almost) COMPLETE HISTORY of the Doctor

I've racked up quite a few different faces now, so it's no great surprise that I sometimes run into some of the old favourites on my travels. There are a lot of Doctors out there . . .

## PART 3

### DOCTORS ASSEMBLE!

Sometimes, when a threat is very great, it takes more than one of me to see it off. When Omega (an ancient, powerful and very threatening Time Lord) turned up after being presumed dead, my two previous faces were plucked out of time to help me. The Time Lords were so grateful, they lifted my exile. But then my third incarnation's travels were cut short when he got radiation poisoning while trying to defeat a load of giant spiders. Here we go again!

FIRST CONTACT SONTARANS

### SCARF ACE

Time for another facelift – and this next guy was one of my absolute favourites. I might even become him again in the future, which would be amazing. Big curly hair, massive teeth and a scarf you could trip up a Cyberman with. Now that's what I call a Doctor.

FIRST CONTACT ZYGONS

### HOMECOMING

Around this time, I got a very important signal: a recall, summoning me back home to Gallifrey. The Master was there too, looking like he'd been left out in the sun too long. It reminded me that my real place wasn't there – it was in my TARDIS, having adventures.

## FLUX FIXER

Unjumble the words mixed up by the Flux . . .

### DOZEN HEAT

CLUE: dangerous games!

Answer on page 61

## FIVE DOCTORS

It seems like every time I pop back to Gallifrey, I learn some awful secret about a terrible thing that happened there a long time ago. That's what happened when someone reactivated the Death Zone – a deadly playground where Time Lords used to drop other races and make them fight to the death. This time, it was previous Doctors who ended up there. I'm not sure what was harder work – figuring out who was behind it all or keeping my other selves from squabbling!

**FIRST CONTACT**
**RASTON WARRIOR ROBOT**

TURN
TO
PAGE
36

## FULL HOUSE

The TARDIS got very busy around this time – more like an intergalactic flatshare! Well, I was suddenly young and cool, so it made sense to liven things up. I was a bit miffed when a cheeky Terileptil destroyed my sonic screwdriver, though. It took me ages to find half an hour to build another one.

## PET PROJECT

I'd had loads of human friends by then, but I've always been one for new experiences, so I got myself a dog! No ordinary dog, either. K-9 was a robot supercomputer with a laser-gun nose. Very handy to have around – unless we landed somewhere that wasn't all flat surfaces. Trust me to pick a dog with four wheels instead of four legs!

## THE LONG GAME

I was such a fan of this daft old mug that I held on to it for much longer than usual (you get through bodies very rapidly when you live my kind of life!). As ever, the time came to say farewell to one face and hello to the next. If that wasn't bad enough, I had to unravel that brilliant scarf to stop myself getting lost in the TARDIS. I wonder if I've still got the knitting pattern somewhere . . .

> I've been on a few quests in my time, and one thing I've learned is that the treasure at the end isn't necessarily a pot of gold!

# Treasure Hunts

## FLUX MARKS THE SPOT

**THE TREASURE:** The date of the end of the world

**THE QUEST:** Things were bad. The Flux was coming, and the Doctor had been turned into a Weeping Angel. But she'd left me a hologram with special instructions in case we got separated. We knew there was going to be a big battle for the Earth, but not when it was due to happen. My quest was to travel the world with Dan looking for clues until we learned the date of the battle.

**THE OUTCOME:** It took years, but we eventually found a friendly seer in Nepal who had the information we needed. But our quest wasn't over – the date was 5 December 2021, and we were in 1904!

## HUNT FOR THE FUGITIVE

**THE TREASURE:** Ruth Clayton

**THE QUEST:** The Judoon – a gang of space thugs who like to think they are some sort of intergalactic police force, but aren't – came to Earth and started conducting a very thorough search for someone. They put a force field round Gloucester (a city in the west of England), meaning nobody could leave, and started scanning the population. The 'treasure' for the Judoon was a load of reward money if they found the fugitive.

**THE OUTCOME:** This prize turned out to be even more valuable than anyone could have guessed. The woman the Judoon were after, Ruth Clayton, was another Doctor, hiding out on Earth.

## DIVIDED DALEK

**THE TREASURE:** A Dalek mutant
**THE QUEST:** A pair of archaeologists found something unusual buried beneath Sheffield Town Hall, but it was no ordinary treasure. It was one third of a mutant taken from the shell of a Dalek that had fallen to Earth in the ninth century. The humans who captured it realised it was too dangerous to leave in one piece, so they chopped it into three and buried the bits in secret locations.
**THE OUTCOME:** Now revived and whole again, the Dalek squid set out on a treasure hunt of its own to find any piece of its metal shell that'd survived.

## SEARCHING THE SEAS

**THE TREASURE:** The lost treasure of the *Flor de la Mar*
**THE QUEST:** In nineteenth-century Asia, pirate queen Madame Ching was looking for buried treasure, but accidentally unleashed a monstrous alien force. She went head-to-fin with the violent Sea Devil pirate, who had plans of his own for the lost treasure … and for the land-dwelling inhabitants of Earth!
**THE OUTCOME:** It turned out that Ching actually wanted the lost treasure in order to free her crew, who were being held hostage for a ransom. With help from the Doctor, Dan and me, Ching eventually managed to find the loot and free her nautical fam!

## RALLY OF THE TWELVE GALAXIES

**THE TREASURE:** The Ghost Monument
**THE QUEST:** Not long after I met the Doctor, we lost the TARDIS and ended up on Desolation, the venue for the last stage of the Rally of the Twelve Galaxies. The final two competitors had to navigate all the dangers of a very inhospitable planet, with only one goal – becoming the first to reach the Ghost Monument.
**THE OUTCOME:** Funnily enough, the treasure they were looking for and the treasure we were looking for were the same. The TARDIS was the Ghost Monument!

# Clara Oswald and the ENCHANTED forest

### by Jasbinder Bilan

Morning sunshine burst through the window as Clara grabbed her phone from the bedside table. Things had been tough lately. She couldn't do a thing right as far as her mum was concerned – they'd been rowing about the tiniest little detail.

She tapped out a reply to her best friend, Ashari.

> Need to persuade Mum to let me sleep over. Shouldn't be hard!!

Clara couldn't wait for this Halloween party. Not *just* because Ashari had persuaded Gem to go, but he *was* just the loveliest, most thoughtful boy in Year Ten. And pretty cool too – he had dark hair which he wore swept off his beautiful golden face.

Clara looked at herself in the mirror and blew her brown fringe off her own face.

'Hi, Gem,' she practised. 'Fancy seeing you here!'

They had a few classes together but they didn't know each other too well. But what Clara *did* know was that every time she saw him, her legs turned to jelly. The party would be a chance for them to hang out together.

Clara's phone pinged with another message from Ashari.

> Bring your party clothes to mine for 7. Mum's going to drive us.

'Clara!' Her mum called up the stairs. 'You've left the kitchen in a right mess from last night.'

Clara went out on to the landing. 'Keep your hair on, Mum. It's not that bad.'

'Get down here now.'

*Here we go again.* Clara sidled down the stairs.

'Don't talk to me like that,' warned her mum, walking back into the kitchen. She sat down at the table and began reading through some work notes. She glanced at Clara who was still standing in the doorway.

'Sorry.' Clara didn't mean to annoy her mum, today of all days. She was meant to be persuading her to let her sleep over at Ashari's tonight. 'I'll do it now,' she said, as she began loading the dishwasher.

'Mum?'

'Yes?' She carried on reading her notes.

'You know this party I'm going to tonight?'

She looked up, a frown grazing her forehead. 'I didn't know you were going to a party.'

Clara felt her cheeks turn hot. 'I told you last week. It's a Halloween party . . . and *everyone's* sleeping over.'

'Well, not you.'

'You never let me do anything. *Please*. I'm nearly fifteen.'

'I've said no – it's final, Clara. I don't want you sleeping over, especially on Halloween. People do all sorts of things on nights like that.'

'What sorts of things? Like some bloodsucking vampire digging his teeth into my neck?' Clara's words dripped with sarcasm.

'You can go for a couple of hours and your dad'll pick you up, before things get silly.'

'Mum, please!' Hot tears stung Clara's cheeks.

'I'm sorry, Clara, it's for the best.'

Clara slammed the kitchen door and thumped up the stairs to her bedroom. She wanted to show her mum just how upset she was. Picking up a book, the one her mum had read to her every night when she was little, Clara opened the window.

Her mum thundered up the stairs after her and stood in the doorway. 'I'm not changing my mind – it's final.'

Clara held the book in front of her mum and turned the pages until she found the leaf that had brought her parents together all those years ago. It might seem silly, but this leaf was the most important thing to Clara's family – and to Clara.

She picked it out of the book and held it in her trembling hands and, as her mum's eyes widened in shock, Clara let the precious thing fly out into the air.

They both watched as the wind caught the leaf, lifted it into the sky and blew it away.

'Clara!' It was her mum's turn to cry now. 'Clara, how could you?' Her mum ran down the stairs, opened the kitchen door and stared into the sky, but the treasured leaf had vanished.

Clara stuffed her party gear into a bag and slammed out of the house.

*

After school had finished, Clara and Ashari picked up some chips then headed over to Ashari's house. But in the back of her mind Clara knew that throwing the leaf out of the window had been a step too far . . . and it was too late now.

She pushed the sad feelings away and thought about Gem instead. 'He's definitely coming, isn't he?' she asked.

'I told him he had to, otherwise he'd have me to answer to,' laughed Ashari, pushing her fingers through her short, purple-tipped hair. She slotted her key into the front door and shoved it open. 'Quick, let's get upstairs before Dad starts on at us.'

'Is that you, Ashari?'

She popped her head into the sitting room. 'Yeah, Dad – Clara's here. We're going to get ready for Satchen's party.'

Clara followed Ashari to her bedroom. They put on music and started to get ready. Clara pulled out her crumpled dress from the rucksack. She was going for a gothic vampire look, so the creases added to her character.

Clara wriggled into the pink-and-purple sparkly dress and holey tights and pushed her feet into red Doc Martens.

Ashari whistled. 'Here, let me do your make-up.' She carefully loaded blood-red lipstick on to Clara's lips and went heavy with the black eyeliner.

'I'm going for vampire beauty,' said Clara, laughing, 'not Cruella De Ville. Make it look cool!'

Ashari's mum drove them to the gates of the party. The house was at the far edge of town, where the verges were wide and leafy and the houses had vast rambling gardens. It was dark already and the yellow moon poked out through the shadow-shimmer of the clouds.

'Are you sure you'll be OK?' asked Ashari's mum. 'I can take you right in if you like.'

'No, Mum.' Ashari rolled her eyes. 'Here's fine!'

Clara glanced at her phone.

Clara – let me know where you are.

I love you Mum X

Her finger hovered over the text but, instead of replying, Clara ignored her mum's message and shoved the phone away.

*

As Clara and Ashari made their way down the winding driveway, the house – strung with ghoulish bat lights – glowed ahead of them. Clara felt a sudden shiver prickle along her spine and imagined shadows hiding between the darkened branches. When they arrived at the front door a pumpkin screamed silently at them with its menacing mouth.

They followed a PARTY sign gripped in a skeletal hand round to a brick barn deeper inside the garden. Clara knocked on the door and music thumped out into the night as the door opened and they were swallowed into the belly of the party.

It was heaving inside the barn. Clara and Ashari pushed their way through the dancing bodies dressed in all sorts of costumes, and grabbed themselves Cokes from the table laden with scary-faced mini pizzas, sausage rolls and bowls of crisps.

'Look, there's Gem.' Ashari caught hold of Clara's hand and dragged her across to him.

He was dressed as a vampire too, with white dusty make-up and a line of blood dripping from his lips. His hair was gelled back, except for the strand that flopped over his eyes – as usual.

'Hello,' said Clara shyly.

'Hi,' replied Gem, clearing his throat.

The three of them danced together, taking breaks for food and drink until someone suggested a game of hide-and-seek in the woods at the back of the house.

'Come on!' a voice cried. 'If you're brave enough.'

'It's really dark out there,' said Clara.

'You're not scared, are you?' laughed Gem. 'What could happen?'

'He's right,' agreed Ashari. 'The woods aren't big, only a few trees really.'

Before she could think any more about it, Clara was being led out of the barn into the darkness.

*

The forest – to Clara it was more of a forest than a wood – was filled with shifting shadows. Huge branches towered over them, high-pitched chattering sounds echoing to and fro. Clara could still see the house from here, the hazy lights twinkling in the near distance.

'Right, let's play!' someone cried, their voice faint among the crowded trees. 'You're it, Clara.'

'Will you be OK by yourself?' asked Ashari.

'Course,' replied Clara, trying to sound braver than she felt.

'Sure?'

Clara was already scared – she hated being alone – but she couldn't lose face, especially not in front of Gem. 'Yeah, go. I'm counting.'

Gem and Ashari ran to join the dancing group from the barn, their laughter mingling with the low hoots of owls. And another strange sound – the cracking of tree roots.

Clara finished counting to a hundred and opened her eyes. The lonely thrum of her heartbeat pounded in her ears as she swallowed and peered through the thick, dark forest.

The trees loomed around Clara, closing in, their gnarled roots ready to trip her up. Shapes flitted around the forest floor and dreamlike sounds spun their way to her as she tried to push down the fear.

She thought she heard shouts and raced off in their direction until she was in the middle of a clearing, the bright moon beating down on her. But there was nobody here.

She let out a small cry. 'Where's the house?'

Shivers bumped up her spine – all the trees looked the same. The awful truth thumped at her belly. She was already lost.

A sudden memory of the time she got lost on Blackpool beach brought tears to her eyes. But her mum had found her. Mum had said she'd always find her, even if she was on the Moon. She'd made Clara feel so safe. Clara remembered the touch of her palm against her mum's and suddenly wished her mum was here now. She'd

know exactly what to do.

Clara wiped her cheek on her sleeve and told herself to grow up. Her mum was back at home, and anyway . . . Clara didn't know if she'd ever forgive her for losing the precious leaf.

She stared out towards the trees again, their ridged bark running up the trunks in furrows, their gangly branches sharp against the moonlight. A strange cracking sound froze Clara to the spot. They were moving!

She forced herself to stop being melodramatic. Trees didn't move. She blinked, then rubbed her eyes, but she was convinced now that the trees really were creeping towards her. As they got closer, she saw sneering faces on the bark, and her chest tightened.

With each crack of their roots they moved towards Clara. Should she make a run for it, ducking under their branches?

What if they caught her?

Blood pumped fast round her body and she made tight fists, trying to calm herself. But each moment she did nothing, the trees were crowding in. Clara felt a long spiky arm grab hold of her and roots tangle around her legs. She felt paralysed!

She screamed and made a grab for the lower branches of the closest tree, the only one that wasn't moving and wasn't part of this terrifying herd surrounding her.

Clara tried to climb up. Just above her head she saw a hollow in the tree, lit up by moonlight, and slotted her hand in. Using all her strength she thrashed and wriggled herself free of the grappling, grasping

roots of the moving trees.

But they came for her again with their writhing tentacles and tried to trap her once more, whipping their roots along the length of the trunk, using them like ropes to haul themselves up.

Panting for breath, she stretched up, desperate to get away, and continued to climb towards the Moon, diving between the upper branches. But the cracking below was louder and more furious with each step Clara took. She didn't dare look back, and stared ahead instead, her arms trembling as she hoisted herself higher and higher – as if she was climbing up to the stars.

She gasped.

Before her, suspended in the sky, was a blue box, a bit like a phone box but wooden and with a light on top. It was just . . . there, above the forest, in a wave of shimmering white mist. The door was flung open and yellow light shone out from it. *What was this?*

Balancing at the very top of the tree, Clara felt a crooked branch grab for her. It grazed her foot and she screamed. *What should she* do? A tendril began to snake around her ankle.

Clara sensed curious eyes watching her from above, through the canopy of autumn leaves. The blue box seemed to manoeuvre closer, as if it was shifting to help Clara escape the trees.

She shook off the branch and leapt into the open box, gripping the lintel. Trembling, she hauled herself away from the trees and into the unknown.

*

'Who are you?' Clara asked in disbelief, staring at a rather startled-looking man in a fancy red bow tie and tweed jacket. She swallowed.

'Oh! Erm … hello! I'm the Doctor.'

Her mum had always told her not to speak to strange men, and yet here she was. She couldn't help herself, though – it was as if she'd met him before. His big smile and wide eyes seemed so familiar . . . 'Doctor *Who*?'

'Correct – now come in if you're coming,' he said, adjusting his bow tie. 'I'm in the middle of something very clever and fiddly.' He began to poke at a few buttons on an old-fashioned typewriter that made up part of the elaborate controls in front of him and the door closed.

'I was being chased by t-trees.' Clara felt a little silly now.

'Ah yes! Nasty, grabby trees. Big nuisance!' He stared into the deck and his face lit up. 'I *think* those trees might be dormant lifeforms from another planet.'

Clara put her hand over her mouth to stop the giggles.

'Do you mean aliens?!' she said laughing. Suddenly all the fear from earlier flew away.

'I'm glad you've cheered up and yes, aliens, I suppose. I've an idea they were feeding off you somehow. Off your . . . uncertainty.' He looked closely at Clara.

'Mmm.' She took a step back from him and stared around, for the first time properly taking in the room. She felt a sudden tug of nerves. 'But the police box – it looked so small on the outside. How can it be so incredible on the inside?'

The man laughed. 'Magic!' he waved his hands mysteriously. 'Not really. Just a nifty bit of science with a big dollop of imagination. Welcome to the TARDIS. Now where do you want to go? Actually, no, first things first. What's your name?' He looked directly at her again.

Clara reddened. She hesitated, then held her hand towards the Doctor. 'It's Clara, Clara Oswald. Pleased to meet you.'

He crinkled his brow, thinking. 'Clara Oswald? Er – no, I mean not meant to happen now. Got my dates muddled, just wanted to check on you. Should've known it would backfire.'

Clara felt her heart thump. 'You're not making any sense.'

'Sorry. Forget all of that. Pleased to meet you, Clara Oswald the er – vampire!'

Clara had forgotten about her outfit and she blushed again. The evening was getting weirder by the minute.

Suddenly, the phone box lurched to one side. Clara managed to glimpse out of the window as she was thrown towards the doors. Her friends were still down there, calling out to her. The forest was alive around them. The trees were staring up with menacing eyes, clawing at the sky. But it was as though her friends couldn't see the trees – like the only person they wanted was Clara.

Then the phone box lurched again, and the cracking sound of roots being sucked out of the earth became fainter and fainter.

'We're flying away! Take me back!' she shouted, fear gripping her again. 'Please take me back to my friends.'

'I'm doing my best' said the Doctor, yanking at various controls in a flurry of motion. 'But the TARDIS doesn't always do what she's told. It's called the TARDIS by the way.' He grinned at her.

The TARDIS suddenly began to spin wildly, flinging both Clara and the Doctor against the walls. They whirred through the sky as Clara scrambled back to the window, panic gripping her chest. Outside, stars spun past her at flicker-speed and Clara felt like she was drifting further away from everything she knew. She closed her eyes and tried to stop her stomach from turning somersaults.

After what seemed like an eternity but was really only seconds, they finally came to a shuddering stop. They had landed back in the forest.

The door opened and Clara ran out. 'Oh my stars. We're back – and the trees are normal again!' she cried.

The air was fresh and filled with the rich scents of ancient woodland: leaves trodden underfoot, fresh shoots and apple blossom.

Clara couldn't see her friends anywhere. But that didn't matter – she was back. She continued towards the moss-coated trees with leaves as wide as palms.

'Clara!' called the Doctor. 'Come back. I think I might have got my landing a bit off. It's not the same forest!'

But Clara didn't hear. She was caught in the spell of this place. Above her a halo of stars shot against the indigo night and the bright silver moon hung like a delicate fingernail in the sky. In the far-off distance the peaks of snow-capped mountains rose tall as giants.

It was like she was always meant to find this place. She knew this wasn't where she'd left Gem and Ashari, but there was something so familiar and safe about it. She didn't feel frightened, but stepped with wonder through the moon-dappled trees. They were the complete opposite of the ones in the other forest: they welcomed her with warm and loving energy, as if she belonged.

She spotted a shadow ahead and, without quite knowing why, hurried forward, trying to catch up with it.

'Clara, wait!' she heard the Doctor calling behind her. 'I can't keep up! Tweed jackets and pointy branches don't combine well . . . Argh, I'm stuck!' But Clara was already too enchanted to listen.

The white wolf sat waiting for Clara. Its fur silky and fine, its ears alert, listening to the forest hum. It was tucked

into the shadow of a grand tree and when it saw Clara it blinked deep hazeleyes rimmed green and leaf brown.

Clara paused, fear suddenly shooting through her. But the wolf sat still and fixed her again with its eyes like autumn leaves. She felt a familiar tug at her heart and sprinted towards the wolf, throwing her arms around the white body. This was a mother wolf, Clara somehow knew, and she felt her gentle heartbeat against her own. It made no sense, but it was as if they had known each other Clara's whole life.

Rising up, the she-wolf led Clara further into the forest, and together they disappeared into this new world.

\*

The wolf showed Clara a huge hollow tree beside a fast-flowing river . . . just as the first flakes of winter snow began to fall.

The wolf padded across to the hollow and rested on a thick bed of fallen leaves. Clara joined her and placed her head against the comfort of the she-wolf's fur. A memory from long ago wended its way to Clara; she remembered being wrapped safely in a blanket beside her mum, and Mum's voice telling Clara that she would always protect her, no matter what.

An unexpected tear froze on Clara's cheek and then the memory, like a precious diamond, tinkled to the ground.

When Clara looked into the sky, the moon appeared again from between the clouds, lighting up a scooped-out hole in the gnarled branch above her head. She stood on tiptoes and pressed her fingers into the hole. There she found something; something worn smooth by loving hands.

'It's the leaf!' she cried, unbelieving. 'Mum and Dad's leaf.'

She couldn't explain it. She couldn't explain any of this. But she'd found the leaf again, and that was a miracle. Once she got home she'd make it up to her mum. She knew this with certainty, though she couldn't explain why. Clara tucked the leaf safely in her pocket and turned to face the she-wolf again. She was bent over the water that ran smooth and river-green past the hollow tree. It was still snowing and everything was painted an ethereal white.

Clara went to join the she-wolf at the river's edge and together they stared into the water – into their past lives and their future ones.

Looking into the river as it swept across the stones, Clara sensed something else. The Doctor, somehow, in her future. But the thought drifted away under the icy water on its way to a distant sea.

None of it mattered. She let her body fill with a happiness that she'd never really felt before. She knew that

whatever happened everything would be OK. She'd return the leaf and make everything right with her mum.

The she-wolf nudged Clara's hand open and on the sloping banks of the river she dropped something into Clara's outstretched palm.

Clara stared at the piece of bright amber lit by moonlight. It was incredible. Perfectly preserved inside was the most delicate feather.

She was so enthralled with the amber that she didn't see her she-wolf leave, but when she lifted her head to the hollow tree it was empty. She felt her heart patter. A fierce howl echoed through the forest and the word *trust* sprang into Clara's mind.

Her she-wolf must have been as silent as a shadow. Clara saw fresh pawprints marking the snow and hurried to follow. She heard the howl again and ahead of her she saw the she-wolf, raised on her hind legs, facing a snarling sabre-toothed tiger.

The tiger was bigger than the she-wolf, with bronze mottled fur and two immense, dripping canines. It towered above the smaller creature.

Fear snapped at Clara as the tiger pounced at the wolf, batting her to the ground with its powerful paw. The tiger suddenly turned as it spotted Clara, and made to attack. But the she-wolf was between them in a heart-beat. She grew fiercer, her eyes full of fire as she leapt at the sabretooth.

Clara took out the leaf from her pocket and with

shaking hands, held it up to the incredible tiger. If the leaf had brought her parents together, maybe it really did have magical powers. The sabretooth shrank back, turned and miraculously retreated towards the mountains.

'Oh my stars!' she murmured, her heart fluttering like a trapped butterfly. She put the leaf back in her pocket.

The she-wolf led Clara back to the hollow tree and they rested by the river until a yellow haze filled the whole forest. In the near distance, she saw a shape fading in and out of existence, lit golden by the glow. A wheezing, grinding noise floated across the glade.

Something was arriving. Clara had to shield her eyes as a brightness shone out of the object like a thousand suns.

'It's that box again,' breathed Clara. 'And the Doctor.'

\*

The spell was broken. Clara buried her head in the she-wolf's fur. 'Until the next time,' she whispered.

The strange Doctor man who had brought her here was waiting in the entrance of the open TARDIS. He was smiling softly. 'I won't ask what happened here, if you don't want to tell me,' he said, very gently. 'But I have got the TARDIS working again. Want a lift?'

This was amazing! Clara held out her hand and felt a spark pass through it as the Doctor hauled her back inside the glowing TARDIS.

'I'm glad I found you again,' he said, a twinkle in his eye. 'I thought I'd lost you.'

'I had an adventure,' said Clara. 'It was strange but . . . wonderful.'

'And I found this.' Clara fished the autumn leaf from deep inside her pocket. 'It's very special. You won't believe me but it's the exact same leaf that brought my parents together.'

'You'd be surprised by the things I believe, Clara Oswald.'

'I'm so glad I found it. I had a row with Mum this morning and threw it out of the window.'

The Doctor looked sad, suddenly. He straightened his bow tie and cleared his throat. 'Well, that sounds like *quite* a leaf. Keep it safe from now on. You never know when it might come in handy.'

'Definitely.' Clara put the leaf back in her pocket. 'And I met a she-wolf. She gave me this.' She held out the bright piece of amber. 'I think it's maybe thousands of years old.'

'Let me see.' The Doctor examined it with a magnifying glass he'd produced from the inside pocket of his tweed jacket. 'Correction – millions of years old.'

'OK, clever clogs, what sort of bird is the feather from?'

'Not a bird.' He tapped his head. 'A dinosaur!'

'What!' cried Clara, looking over the Doctor's shoulder.

'*This* dinosaur would have lived millions of years ago, a long time before you, Clara. It was the size of a small bird. Probably got trapped in the tree resin while searching for grubs.'

This ancient piece of tree resin that had survived millions of years. Maybe the she-wolf just thought it was a beautiful object. But maybe, just maybe, she was trying to give Clara an important message. That some things are fleeting, but some leave their mark forever. Ancient and indestructible. It was a reminder of the infinity of life.

'OK.' Clara smiled. 'Can I have it back now? I'm going to have it made into a necklace.'

'Good idea! Don't get too attached to it, though – you might lose it.'

'I won't lose it.'

'Just saying – you might. You never know. And anyway, it's OK, we have to let some things go.'

Clara frowned.

'Where shall we go, then?' The Doctor asked quickly, before pushing his hands through his floppy hair like he suddenly regretted asking the question.

He returned to the panel of switches and busied himself, turning them on and off.

In a daze, Clara leant against the wall. 'Is there a kitchen in here? I'd love a cup of tea.'

'Of course! Can't have a spaceship without a kitchen. Mine's milk and two sugars, please.' He looked at her again with that searching gaze.

'I want to go home,' Clara finally said, smiling. 'I can't wait to show Mum I've found her leaf. She'll be so happy.'

As she felt the box lurch once again, sending them into flight, Clara stared in disbelief at how huge the inside of it was. She became wrapped up in its magic once more, all thoughts of tea forgotten.

She felt them spin across the skies, away from the enchanted forest, hurtling through space, until at last it was back in the hide-and-seek woods.

The Doctor brought the ship to a standstill in the same spot where Clara had started to count to a hundred.

She suddenly remembered her friends – they must be so worried. While she'd been off having an adventure they'd probably been searching the woods looking for her. She sprang to the door and pushed it open.

'Thanks for the ride,' she called.

'Nice to meet you again, Clara Oswald.' The Doctor gave her a mysterious look – sort of sad and happy at the same time. 'Now, Clara, listen.'

As she stopped and faced the Doctor, Clara felt that strange sensation again – that she knew this man, somehow.

'So we *have* met before?'

'This is going to sound weird. We'll meet again in the future and have *so many* adventures, I promise, but for now I need you to forget.'

'What?'

He placed a hand on Clara's temple, ever so gently.

'You won't recall any of this trip. You'll forget you ever met me.'

Clara felt like she was falling into a dream, a buzzing sound travelling through her body and brain.

*

When she opened her eyes, she was in the woods beside the huge oak tree, its branches towering above her into the night sky.

'Come on, Clara.' It was Gem. 'What took you so long? We all got tired of waiting and I came to find *you* instead.'

Clara smiled.

'Where did you get to?' said Ashari, appearing from between the trees.

Clara rubbed her eyes and yawned. 'I don't know what happened. I must have fallen asleep.'

In a daze, her fingers found the leaf and amber nestled in her pocket. For a fleeting moment she remembered something . . . and then, like the best dreams, it flew away into the stars.

A short story from the upcoming collection

BBC DOCTOR WHO

ORIGIN STORIES
In stores September 2022

# The (Almost)
# COMPLETE HISTORY *of the Doctor*

After a pretty decent unbroken run of adventures, it was time for me to have a bit of a rest. But don't worry, I wasn't about to vanish forever! A universe without the Doctor? What a terrible idea!

## PART 4

### LONG LIVE THE QUEEN

My next persona bit the dust on a trip to the desert planet of Androzani with my new friend, Peri. We both got poisoned, and the only cure was the milk of a queen bat that lived deep in an underground cave system. There wasn't any left for me after Peri had hers, so it was time to change again . . .

### IT'S A LOOK

Usually, my personality stabilises quickly after a regeneration, but unfortunately for poor Peri, I was a handful for quite a while after this one. (Sorry, Peri.) My choice of clothing has often been the talk of the galaxy, but my signature look around this time was particularly brash. I loved everything about it – and the rainbow I wear now is my little tribute to this Doctor's colourful taste.

FIRST CONTACT MENTORS

### ON TRIAL!

As well as fighting monsters and sorting out fair play across the universe, this Doctor was also put on trial by the Time Lords. They had a cheek putting anyone on trial, frankly, considering some of the stuff they've got up to themselves. There was a major twist when it turned out the prosecutor was basically another version of me! The Valeyard claimed to be made up of all the dark bits of my nature. Honestly, the multiverse has got a lot to answer for.

FIRST CONTACT VERVOIDS

## FLUX FIXER

Unjumble the words mixed up by the Flux . . .

**ELVA HYDRATE**

CLUE: another me?

Answer on page 61

## THE WILDERNESS YEARS

After that, everything went a bit quiet for a while. There are no visual records of any of my adventures for a long time – although there are written archives. Don't worry though – I was still out there, fighting monsters and keeping the universe in order.

## ABOUT TIME

Just as suddenly as I vanished, I was back! New face, new adventures and a very cool new look for the inside of my TARDIS. I got bored of it being white, and transformed it into something more like a grand cathedral. I also got some lamps and candles for the first time, which was wonderful. I might never have the big light on again!

TURN TO PAGE 44

## THE ARCH MANIPULATOR

I was also a bit of a schemer back then. I once managed to trick the Daleks into destroying their own home planet, and I got the Cybermen to wipe out an entire battle fleet. Having said that, I was strongly anti-violence – something that has stayed with me ever since.

**FIRST CONTACT HAEMOVORES**

## BIKE BOTHER

When I regenerate, I like to go out in a blaze of glory – fireworks, TARDIS collapsing around me, that sort of thing. But this time, I was caught off guard, and ended up changing after I fell off my exercise bike. Well, they can't all be spectacular, I suppose.

**FIRST CONTACT TETRAPS**

## DOCTOR WHO?

If you think I'm mysterious now, you should have met this version of me. He was textbook mysterious: always dropping little hints that he wasn't the person everyone thought he was. He had a jumper with loads of question marks dotted around, so maybe he just took that theme and ran with it.

# FACT OR FIB?

There's a lot of chatter about me, my friends and my enemies around the universe, but sometimes people get their facts mixed up. Can you tell which of these statements are true and which are false?

The Sontarans are a clone race.
FACT 1 FIB

Yaz used to be a trainee police officer.
FACT 2 FIB

Swarm and Azure are husband and wife.
FACT 3 FIB

Kate Stewart is the head of UNIT.
FACT 4 FIB

Karvanista used to work for the Grand Serpent.
FACT 6 FIB

The Master is the Doctor's brother.
FACT 5 FIB

The Doctor's home planet is called Time.
FACT 7 FIB

Answers on page 61

# The Doctor's
# FAMILY ALBUM PART 3

## PERI BROWN

Poor old Peri. She thought she was heading off on the ultimate gap year with a handsome young stranger (me, when I was a lad!). Then somehow, she ended up married to a warrior king with a giant beard who shouted a lot. Funny how things turn out, eh?

## SARAH JANE SMITH

One of my most faithful friends of all – Sarah Jane was by my side through three different faces (and popped up to visit a few more besides!). She was one of the country's top journalists, and her eagerness to get to the bottom of a story was one of her greatest assets. We teamed up again after many years apart and she had such a blast that she decided to start having adventures with her own incredible gang – protecting the Earth from an attic in Ealing!

## NYSSA

This very regal young lady had to grow up fast when her dad was killed by my archenemy, the Master. Her dad's body was stolen by the Master to replace his own, worn-out one. It must have been so hard for her to see this monster looking like her own dad.

## ROMANA

It's not often I travel with fellow Time Lords – mainly because I kind of like being the smartest person in the room. But I made an exception for Romana. She had two different faces while she was with me – she regenerated like other people change their socks.

## ADRIC

Oh, Adric. So young and so clever. I wish every single day that I could have saved his life but he died trying to save Earth.

## DONNA NOBLE

I like to think I can see a bit of me in all my mates, but that was especially true in Donna's case. After absorbing a massive dose of my DNA from a chopped-off spare hand (it's a long story!), she became part Doctor, part Donna. But a human brain isn't built for that – it would have overloaded and killed her. I had to hide all her memories of me. So sad!

39

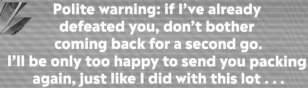

Polite warning: if I've already defeated you, don't bother coming back for a second go. I'll be only too happy to send you packing again, just like I did with this lot . . .

## TZIM-SHA

Ah, my old mate Tim Shaw. (Pretty sure that's how you spell it, anyway.) Tim didn't exactly catch me at my best when we first met – I'd just regenerated, so half my cells were still on the boil. He was a Stenza trophy hunter who killed innocent people for sport, taking out their teeth and embedding them in his own ugly mug. I put a stop to that by teleporting him into exile on the planet Ranskoor Av Kolos, where he spent his time plotting payback.

His revenge plan involved using a telepathic race called the Ux to create a planet-trapping weapon. After testing it out on five unlucky worlds, he turned it on the one whose demise he knew would hurt me most of all: Earth. With the help of my old friends Graham and Ryan, I stopped Tim, saved Earth, and even returned the other five planets to normal. Result!

# REVENGE IS

## THE DALEKS

To be fair, I can understand why the Daleks would want revenge on me. I've personally blown up Skaro, their home planet, at least twice. But I was still miffed when a squad of Executioner Daleks appeared to exterminate me.

They got their eyestalks in a twist after their entire war fleet was wiped out by the Flux. Yes, the Flux was unleashed with the sole aim of obliterating me and wiping out a universe that had my interfering fingerprints all over it, but you can hardly blame me for that. And the plan that brought about the fleet's destruction was thought up by the Sontarans – I just hijacked it. So, I think they were very harsh.

As for coming up with a whole new gun stick designed to bypass my sonic screwdriver (which I created to bypass the effects of their old gun stick)? Just rude.

Anyway, the Daleks thought they were tracking us, so we tricked them into following fake signals, giving us time to blow 'em all up!

## SWARM AND AZURE

Swarm and Azure were sworn enemies of the Division, the secret organisation I was in during a time in my life I can't remember. The early Time Lords wanted to bind time and control it, but Swarm and Azure preferred chaos. The Division sent an earlier version of me to capture them. The result? Swarm was imprisoned in a containment chamber, while Azure was hidden on Earth as a human.

They escaped and set about trying to reach the Division – and me. They took humans who had lost their planets to the Flux, then harvested them for psychotemporal energy.

What did they want that for? To build a bridge to where I was having a showdown with Tecteun (in between universes – cool place for a showdown).

They killed Tecteun before she could reveal the secrets of my past, then tortured me in a loop of my own forgotten memories. But their plan to redirect the Flux ultimately failed, and they were disintegrated by the physical embodiment of time itself.

# SWEET!

## THE MASTER

I've known the Master for a very long time, and he's tried to get his own back on me loads. But his ultimate revenge was for something I didn't even know had happened – something he learned made him lay waste to our home planet and kill every single person on it. And, as far as he was concerned, it was all my fault.

The Master had discovered that part of him existed because of me and the secrets that Tecteun had discovered from the Timeless Child. Every single Time Lord's DNA was based on mine, thanks to the gene splice that gave Gallifreyans the power of regeneration. The idea that any part of him existed because of me sent him totally mad.

# FUR

Be alert – that cute stray dog the little old lady next door is feeding biscuits to could be a very dangerous alien!

**LOOKS LIKE:**

## DOG

**ACTUALLY:**

## LUPARI

Don't be throwing sticks and expecting the Lupari to play fetch. They're a ferociously proud warrior race with an intergalactic space fleet.

## FLUX FIXER

*Unjumble the word mixed up by the Flux . . .*

SUNI RAILS

**CLUE:** reptile rulers.

Answer on page 61

# AND WIDE

**LOOKS LIKE:**
## BAT
**ACTUALLY:**
## TETRAP

There's nowhere to hide when the Tetraps are around – they have eyes in the backs of their heads! And, if you meet a friendly one who looks like he's leaning in for a kiss, beware of his poisonous forked tongue!

**LOOKS LIKE:**
## CAT
**ACTUALLY:**
## CATKIND

These devious felines evolved in the far future and were a big deal on New Earth. One group, the Sisters of Plenitude, were brilliant nurses. But Catkind don't always use their knowledge for good.

**LOOKS LIKE:**
## RHINO
**ACTUALLY:**
## JUDOON

Super-evolved rhinos who have found their niche working as police officers and bounty hunters – jobs very well suited to their stubborn, orderly, rule-obsessed nature! Don't break off a Judoon's horn – the Doctor did that once by accident, and they really didn't like it.

**LOOKS LIKE:**
## FLY
**ACTUALLY:**
## TRITOVORE

If it looks like an insect head on a human body, it's a Tritovore. This advanced species use spaceships for trading expeditions. They feed on the 'waste products' of other species – yes, that does mean poo. Gross!

**LOOKS LIKE:**
## TURTLE
**ACTUALLY:**
## SEA DEVIL

Before humans came along, the Earth was ruled by large reptiles. The ones on land were called Silurians, and the aquatic ones earned the nickname Sea Devils. They all went to sleep to avoid extinction, and any that wake up are usually furious to see us humans wandering around their planet.

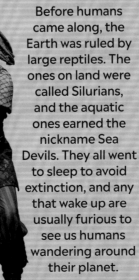

**LOOKS LIKE:**
## SPIDER
**ACTUALLY:**
## RACNOSS

When the Earth was formed, the Racnoss hid right in the centre of the planet and went into hibernation. Billions of years later, they sent a signal to their empress, who rocked up in the sky above London to summon her babies to eat all the humans!

# The (Almost) COMPLETE HISTORY of the Doctor

> The Time War changed everything for me, and made me question whether or not I could even be the Doctor any more. But some brilliant people came into my lives and gave me back my mojo!

## PART 5

### THE WARRIOR

The Fugitive isn't the only Doctor who has appeared out of thin air. With the Time War raging, I crash-landed on the planet Karn and died. Yup, really died. The Sisterhood of Karn – feisty sort of nuns from my own planet who'd set up a home on Karn – brought me back. They said I had to help end the war, but I couldn't do that as the Doctor. So, I became the Warrior. Didn't really want anyone to know though, so I kept it secret for a long time.

### RUN!

When the war was over, I was very glad to be the Doctor again and get back to doing Doctor-y things, such as meeting new friends, travelling the universe and having wonderful adventures. It was just fantastic when I met the brilliant Rose Tyler. Some living plastic creatures turned up in the basement of the shop she worked in, so I grabbed her by the hand, and we started running. After that, we never wanted to stop.

### THE LAST SURVIVOR

Not long after I met Rose, she demanded to know why I was so moody all the time, so I decided to share my secret – that I was the last of the Time Lords, and that all the others had perished in the Time War. I was all on my own. Or so I thought . . .

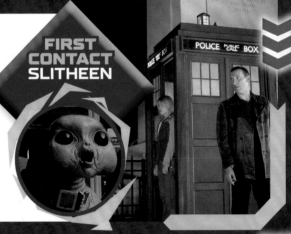

FIRST CONTACT SLITHEEN

POLICE PUBLIC BOX

### BAD WOLF

Everywhere Rose and I went, we kept seeing two words: Bad Wolf. Nobody knew what that meant, until Rose stared into the Time Vortex and became an all-powerful goddess. She took those words off a random wall and scattered them through space and time to lead herself to that moment. But humans aren't supposed to be all-powerful goddesses, so I had to absorb all the power – which kicked off yet another regeneration.

## FLUX FIXER

**Unjumble the words mixed up by the Flux . . .**

**BOWL FAD**

**CLUE:** A message from a friend.

Answer on page 61

### RIVER'S RUN

Around this time, I met the mysterious and fabulous River Song. She was an archaeologist who knew all about me, but I'd never met her. We were moving in opposite directions in our lives. Each time we met, I was older and she was younger. So, the first time we met for me was the last for her. Complicated!

### TIME'S UP

When Davros, creator of the Daleks, came up with a horrific plan to wipe out all of creation, I knew who to turn to for help – my brilliant friends! Even Rose made it back via the Void to lend a hand. It was a brilliant triumph. But I soon learned that another life would be coming to an end . . .

TURN TO PAGE 50

### YOU ARE NOT ALONE

Remember how I thought I was the only Time Lord left? Well, that wasn't true. I met a bloke called Professor Yana. Nice old guy – or so I thought. The professor had a fob watch, just like the one Tecteun used to store my stolen life. Only the professor's contained the memories of someone I knew very well. He. Was. The Master!

**FIRST CONTACT
WEEPING ANGELS**

### PARALLEL LIVES

My new face and Rose got on brilliantly and had lots of incredible escapades together. But Rose started getting worried after she met my old companion Sarah Jane Smith. Like Rose, Sarah thought she'd be with me forever, but Time Lords and humans have very different lives – and lifespans.

**FIRST CONTACT
OOD**

### DOOMSDAY

Sure enough, Rose and I were torn apart. She was pulled across the Void – the space between parallel universes – to another version of Earth. That was somewhere even the TARDIS couldn't go, so I was on my own again. New friends came and went, including marvellous Martha and hilarious Donna, but nobody was quite like Rose.

# THE FLUX
# FOES

Not everyone we met during the Flux was sound. I wouldn't go out of my way to see any of this lot again . . .

## WEEPING ANGELS

The Doctor had met these stony-faced frighteners before, so we knew we were in trouble from the off. They survive by whizzing people back in time and living off the time energy of the life they would have lived. Usually, you need to see an Angel for it to get you. But, as a woman called Claire Brown discovered, they can also capture you if you have a premonition of one.

I had my own Angel issues when me and Yaz went to the village of Medderton in 1967. Just one touch from an Angel was all it took to send us back to 1901, where we had to find a way to get back to our own time. And, with no TARDIS around, it took us a good few years to get there!

## FLUX FIXER

**Unjumble the word mixed up by the Flux . . .**

**RAG SAVER**

**CLUE:** what Swarm and Azure were.

Answer on page 61

# SWARM

Swarm was a Ravager – an ancient creature who liked messing about with time. He'd spent billions of years in captivity, plotting revenge on the Doctor, who'd put him there. After breaking out, he was reunited with his sister, Azure, and the pair of them headed straight for the Temple of Atropos to start tampering with the fabric of time.

Swarm wasn't keen on time proceeding in any kind of order. He was all for unleashing it and having everything happening all at once. Like the telly playing every channel at the same time. He thought he was the puppet master of the whole Flux thing, but the Doctor stayed one step ahead.

# AZURE

Azure might look like a shiny festive bauble but, trust me, you wouldn't want her hanging off your Christmas tree. For a start, she could turn living things to ash with a single touch – just like her brother.

This terrible two could teleport anywhere in space and time, and form psychic links between themselves and others. They combined these skills to get to where the Doctor was, for a final confrontation. What the Ravagers didn't know was that the Doctor had been splintered into three versions of herself, all working separately to defeat them. No contest!

# PASSENGER

Passenger wasn't strictly bad, but it was certainly put to some dodgy uses by Swarm and Azure. It was shaped like a human but that's where the similarity ended. It was a walking prison, designed to hold millions of people captive at once.

The Ravagers used Passenger to capture survivors of the Flux. Azure lied to them, telling them that they would be transported to safety, but they were used as hostages. Passenger did come in handy for one thing in the end, though – the Doctor used it to contain what was left of the Flux.

# THE GRAND SERPENT

This Grand Serpent fella was a sneaky one. He came from Vinder's home planet and was a powerful politician there. But at some point he ended up on Earth, where he plotted and schemed to get himself made the big boss of UNIT, a branch of the military dedicated to stopping alien threats. Yeah, I know, an alien in charge of the anti-alien task force. You couldn't make it up, could you?

The Grand Serpent – or Prentis, as he was known on Earth – appeared human, but had one very nasty party trick. He could summon up a great big snake creature that would gob its way out of his victims, suffocating them from the inside out.

# UNIT's ULTIMATE

U.N.I.T

DALEKS **VS** SEA DEVILS

**MY PICK**

SONTARANS **VS** PASSENGER

**MY PICK**

**MY PICK**

CYBERMEN **VS** LUPARI

**MY PICK**

**VS** **MY PICK**

WEEPING ANGELS **VS** JUDOON

**MY PICK**

**MY PICK**

**FINAL**

## THE ULTIMATE THREAT IS...

# SHOWDOWN

Attention, all UNIT agents! It's time to compile our Deadly Danger Index to find the most dangerous creature that threatens Earth. Use the intel you've gained from reading this annual to identify the most dangerous threats to Earth from each pair, then write your answer in the box. You'll find monsters on the left and humanoids on the right. Choose wisely – the safety of Earth could depend on it!

*Kate Stewart*
**Head of UNIT**

SWARM **VS** TZIM-SHA

**MY PICK**

**MY PICK**

AZURE **VS** THE MASTER

**MY PICK**

**MY PICK**

**VS**

GRAND SERPENT **VS** DAVROS

**MY PICK**

**MY PICK**

TECTEUN **VS** MADAME CHING

**MY PICK**

**MY PICK**

**BATTLE**

# The (Almost) COMPLETE HISTORY of the Doctor

> Some people believe there's a higher power out there, pulling the strings of life. Well, if I have someone like that, they liked to keep things very wibbly-wobbly around this time . . .

## PART 6

### RAGGEDY DOCTOR

Everything changed again, especially my chin. Look at it – it's magnificent! The first face my new face saw belonged to Amelia Pond, a little girl who was very worried about a crack in her bedroom wall. That crack appeared again and again, everywhere we went. But what lay beyond it? And why did I now like eating fish fingers in custard?

### THREE'S A CROWD

Once Amy had grown up – a few minutes later for me, but longer for her – she came travelling with me, and brought her fiancé, Rory. Later, Amy was swapped for a living slime duplicate. The real Amy had a baby, who was kidnapped. The baby grew up to be River Song, who I married. Happy families!

FIRST CONTACT THE SILENCE

### TOUCHED BY AN ANGEL

It was an encounter with the Weeping Angels that saw me parted from the Ponds. Rory was sent back in time by an Angel, and Amy made sure the Angel got her too so she could join Rory. They lived a long and happy life together, but I didn't get to share it. I was so upset that I parked the TARDIS in some clouds and hid out there for a while.

FLUX FIXER

Unjumble the word mixed up by the Flux . . .

LED NORA

CLUE: a faithful friend.

Answer on page 61

### THE IMPOSSIBLE GIRL

River Song's timeline was complicated, but Clara Oswald's was something else. First, she'd been turned into a Dalek. Then, she was Victorian nanny. Finally, she turned up in twenty-first century London. Why did the same person keep appearing? Because she made it happen! Clara jumped into my timeline, meaning she was around to help every version of me, all at once - including the Warrior. Which set off a very important chain of events . . .

## THE VAULT

Clara went off to do her own thing, so I made a new life on Earth, working at a university, tutoring my new friend Bill Potts, and being irritated by my manservant, Nardole. There was a reason behind my lifestyle change: I had Missy locked away in a vault under the campus. I wanted her to change and become a force for good. But one of her previous faces turned up, so it was two Masters against one Doctor.

## THE END?

Thanks to a direct hit from a Cyberman, I was dying again. But I held in the regeneration energy and refused to change. I was tired, sad and had lost too many people I loved. Meanwhile, at the North Pole, another Doctor was doing the same thing – that old guy who stole the TARDIS and went exploring. Together, we came to terms with our need to change. Time for a new future . . .

**TURN TO PAGE 56**

## ENTER MISSY

Just like Peri all those years ago, it took Clara a while to get used to my new ways. The best way to describe my new personality was 'a bit grumpy'. The Master also reappeared, except he was now she, and had taken the name Missy. She was Scottish, just like me. Maybe all that gene splicing Tecteun did had left us in sync.

**FIRST CONTACT THE MONKS**

## TIME WAR NO MORE

With timelines unravelling, I found myself plunged back into the last day of the Time War, when I destroyed all the Time Lords and Daleks to end the fighting. I never liked that ending, so my selves – two Doctors and the Warrior – came together to rewrite it. Gallifrey was saved and the Daleks were destroyed. The war was over, just in a different way. I hid Gallifrey, one second out of time, to make sure things stayed peaceful.

## CHRISTMAS DAYS

Popping Gallifrey in a pocket universe caused some problems. The Time Lords tried to force their way out, causing the crack in little Amelia Pond's bedroom. The Daleks chased this crack to the town of Christmas on Trenzalore, so I stood guard for hundreds of years. But I was out of lives – until Clara persuaded the Time Lords to post me new regeneration energy through the crack. I used the leftovers to destroy the Daleks and save Christmas!

# SEA-ING DOUBLE

Oi! Stop sniggering at my pirate outfit and help me out for a minute. Now, I'm a pretty observant guy, but there are eight differences between these two pictures and I can only spot one of 'em. Look closely and see if you can work out which squares are different in the second picture. I've filled in the one I got to start you off. Good luck!

1 C1   2 ⬤   3 ⬤
4 ⬤   5 ⬤   6 ⬤

Answers on page 61

# The Doctor's FAMILY ALBUM PART 4

## THE PONDS

This is one complicated family tree. I met Amy, who was engaged to Rory, but Rory died, then came back – as a Roman soldier, waaaay back in time – then Amy died, but she came back too. They got married and had a baby called Melody, who was a child of the TARDIS and could regenerate – which she did, into River Song. And then I married River Song, meaning Amy is my mother-in-law! Phew!

## BILL POTTS

My absolute top priority is making sure bad things don't happen to the people in my care, but that went badly wrong when I was travelling with brilliant Bill Potts. Poor Bill was turned into a Cyberman, and I had no way of changing her back. Luckily, a puddle she had fallen in love with restored her to life (I'm simplifying, but that's the gist of it).

## STEVEN TAYLOR

Steven had been trapped on a dangerous planet for two years before he managed to stow away with me. Along the way, many friends of ours died, and Steven found that hard. But eventually he found his place in the universe, helping two warring societies live peacefully.

## DODO CHAPLET

Loved this cheeky minx. Wandered in, had a few laughs, then just wandered off again. We should all be more Dodo.

## ACE

Ace was always equipped with two things: loads of attitude and an exploding deodorant can filled with Nitro 9. A time storm blew her from her bedroom in London to a supermarket on board a spaceship, which is where we first met. She was a bit rough round the edges when I invited her on board the TARDIS, but, after some training from me, she was ready to take on the universe!

## ZOE HERIOT

Queen of STEM! There wasn't much Zoe didn't know about how things worked.

53

# REGENERATION

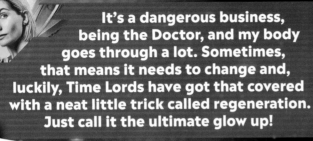

It's a dangerous business, being the Doctor, and my body goes through a lot. Sometimes, that means it needs to change and, luckily, Time Lords have got that covered with a neat little trick called regeneration. Just call it the ultimate glow up!

Regenerating is quite a violent process, so I try to avoid doing it too often. Every cell in my body starts to fizz and boil, transforming into something completely new. Any damage is undone, but I become someone else entirely. Luckily, I get to keep all my old memories, so I'm still the same old Doctor underneath.

For ages, the Time Lords liked people to think that the power to regenerate was their special gift. They reckoned it wasn't a good idea for anyone to live forever, so set a limit of twelve regenerations per Time Lord.

But I've now found out that gift wasn't theirs to give – it was mine. When Tecteun saw little me transform for the first time, she schemed to unlock my secret so she could steal it for herself and then pass it on to other people on Gallifrey.

When it's time to go, there's a great big burst of energy – and you really don't want to be in the room when that happens, as I'm not in control and it can be extremely dangerous.

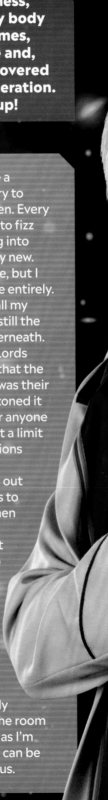

I don't usually get to pick what I'll be when I regenerate, but maybe you can help me out. What would your dream Doctor be like?

**My Doctor's personality is . . .**

. . . . . . . . . . . . . . . . . . . . . . . . . . . . . . . . . . . . .

. . . . . . . . . . . . . . . . . . . . . . . . . . . . . . . . . . . . .

. . . . . . . . . . . . . . . . . . . . . . . . . . . . . . . . . . . . .

**My Doctor's catchphrase is . . .**

. . . . . . . . . . . . . . . . . . . . . . . . . . . . . . . . . . . . .

. . . . . . . . . . . . . . . . . . . . . . . . . . . . . . . . . . . . .

I like to wear clothes that reflect my personality, and I love a few accessories, so don't forget to draw some of those. Here are a few things I've worn in the past to get you thinking . . .

# The (Almost) COMPLETE HISTORY of the Doctor

Time to bring this history bang up to date with a quick run-through of everything I've been up to most recently. This all happened over hundreds of years for me, but it didn't take as long for Yaz . . .

## PART 7

### DOWN TO EARTH

I'm finally me – yay! That took a while, didn't it? And, while all my transformations have been a bit special, this one was particularly brilliant – I am now a woman! I didn't have much time to dwell on this, though, because I was quite literally launched straight into action out of the TARDIS doors – in mid-air! A good way to focus the mind.

### SHEFFIELD STEEL

Fortunately for me, I landed in exactly the right place: Sheffield. If I hadn't, I'd never have met my brilliant Fam: Yaz, Ryan and Graham. They helped me recover from my regeneration and assisted me in picking a very cool new outfit (charity-shop chic!).

### ROSA

I've always warned my friends about the dangers of interfering with established events in history – you can never be too careful. But nasty time-meddler Krasko didn't see things that way. We had to stop him causing chaos in Earth's timeline by making sure Rosa Parks took her seat on a particular bus, one day in December 1955.

CLEVELAND AVE.

### FLUX FIXER

**Unjumble the words mixed up by the Flux . . .**

CELT ROGUES

CLUE: Judoon destination.

Answer on page 61

FIRST CONTACT PTING

### TEAM TARDIS

With my Fam firmly established, we got on with the important business of adventure. Along the way, we ran into a nasty businessman called Jack Robertson, who was involved with some larger-than-life spiders; we visited Yaz's grandparents during the Partition of India; we sorted out some robot bother at a giant warehouse; and we got accused of witchcraft in seventeenth-century Lancashire!

## THE FLUX

Yaz and I spent the next while travelling alone and became a tight unit. But there's always room for one more on the TARDIS, and we were both thrilled when Dan Lewis joined us. Yaz spent years with him while I was sorting out the Flux, so I knew he had to be a good egg!

## THE END . . .

The trouble with being the Doctor is you never know when your time is going to be up. Soon, someone totally different will be standing there in your clothes, looking really confused. This was meant to be the complete story of my life, but really there's no such thing for me. I might never get to write the ending. But that's fine. Who needs endings, anyway? I just want to carry on being the Doctor!

## PRISONER

The Judoon, realising that I was a version of the person they wanted, chucked me in space jail for hundreds of years. Yaz was not best pleased! But there was no time for arguing. Jack Robertson was back in business, making Daleks! Once we'd sorted that out, Graham and Ryan decided to go home.

FIRST CONTACT RAVAGERS

## ON THE RUN

During a visit to Gloucester, we encountered a platoon of Judoon, who were in pursuit of an Earth woman called Ruth Clayton. Except she wasn't an Earth woman: she had a Time Lord biodata module watch stashed away, and when she opened it her true self was revealed. But you know the rest of that from Part 1 of this story. (Unless you're reading my history backwards, of course, which is exactly the kind of thing I would do.)

## IDENTITY CRISIS

After the Master destroyed the Time Lords and revealed some of the details of my secret history, I started to question who I was, and what my place in the universe might be. The Fam realised there was something bothering me – especially Yaz – but I chose to keep it to myself. Still not sure that was the right thing to do.

# NO REGRETS

Why sign up for a life of deadly danger, exploring the darkest corners of the universe, far away from my family and friends? Easy! Because I get to do it all with the Doctor at my side. Here are some of our most amazing moments together . . .

The very first time I met the Doctor, I wasn't sure we were going to get on. I called her 'Madam', and she called me useless! I was a trainee police officer, and she had just fallen straight out of the sky into my life. It was my job to keep order in a dangerous situation, and I don't know if you've noticed but the Doctor isn't a very easy person to control! But, within minutes, she'd announced we were friends, and that was OK by me.

I did think the Doctor was dressed slightly strangely when she first appeared, but I later found out that's because she'd just been a man and was still wearing his clothes! She still managed to do a giant leap between two cranes though, which was impressive. I suggested a shopping trip, and she tried on all sorts of weird and wonderful things before settling on a look that's absolutely perfect for her.

One of the greatest things about having a time traveller for a best mate is that you can peep at events from your family history. Thanks to the Doctor, I had the chance to go back to the Punjab in 1947 and see my grandmother get married. A broken watch revealed a family secret that had been hidden for a very long time – my gran was marrying someone who wasn't my grandad. A different broken watch would later reveal secrets of the Doctor's family tree, so that's another thing we have in common.

When you're used to living an amazing life with the Doctor, being separated from her is the worst thing you can imagine – and it's happened to me more than once. First time was when the Judoon took her off to space prison. We didn't know that's what had happened, so I spent months trying to work out where she might be. The rest of the Fam thought it was time to give up, but how could I ever do that?

We were separated again during the time of the Flux. I was sent off with Dan to search for an important clue, and we were gone for years. Actual years. Can you imagine how hard that was for me, not being able to see the Doctor for all that time? Luckily, she'd given me something to help – a hologram version of herself. Even though she wasn't really there, I felt closer to her when I watched it.

It hasn't all been sadness and separation. We've had some right laughs as well, even though the Doctor can be the most annoying person at times. She's got a gob on her, and often ends up making a sticky situation even worse – like when Karvanista had the pair of us hanging upside down above a sea of boiling acid. As usual, the Doctor came up with a brilliant way for us to escape. It's impossible for me to stay mad at her.

I suppose my feelings for the Doctor have got deeper over the years, without me even properly realising it. It took Dan about ten seconds to guess. But I'm a human and she's basically immortal, so she's right – this is one story that might never have a happy ending. But that doesn't mean I can't enjoy every second while it lasts!

# The Doctor's FAMILY ALBUM

### PART 5

## CLARA OSWALD

Usually, the story about how I met someone is quite simple. But not in Clara's case! Nothing about her was simple. That's why I called her the Impossible Girl. I met her for the first time on three different occasions – splinters of her were scattered all through my timeline. That means she's seen all my faces, and possibly even a few I've forgotten!

## TEGAN JOVANKA

I like to think that, given the choice between a boring old life on Earth and travelling through time with me, most people would be running into the TARDIS without a second thought. Not Tegan! All she seemed to be interested in was getting to Heathrow to start her shift as cabin crew. I did tell her she was welcome to come round the TARDIS every thirty minutes with hot drinks and snacks, but that didn't go down very well. After I managed to get her to the airport, she tracked me down and demanded to come back on board the TARDIS! There's no pleasing some people. I was secretly glad she did, though. Tegan was excellent.

## WILFRED MOTT

Wonderful Wilf was Donna Noble's grandad. After she forgot all about me, he stepped up to help me in her place. There wasn't much that could knock Wilf off his stride – he even tried to take out a Dalek with a paint gun!

## YASMIN KHAN & DAN LEWIS

And of course I haven't forgotten my current crew. Dan's one of the kindest, most generous blokes on Earth (or any other planet he happens to be on). And watching Yaz grow into a truly magnificent human has been one of the greatest joys of all my lives.

## VICKI

A bright girl from the future who settled down in ancient Greece! (That's her on the left, by the way!)

## NARDOLE

Can't believe I'd lived all those lives and it had never occurred to me to get a butler before. Loved having a butler! Of course, Nardole was so much more than that . . .

# PUZZLE ANSWERS

**PAGE 9 Flux Fixer**
*ANSWER* Gallifrey

**PAGE 12 Find the Friends**

Yaz appears **10** times.
Dan appears **7** times.
Sarah appears **7** times.
Nick appears **6** times.

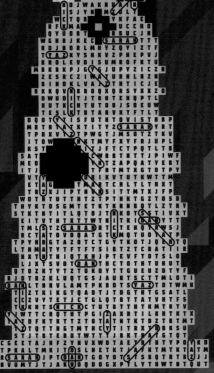

**PAGE 16 Flux Fixer**
*ANSWER* Regeneration

**PAGE 19 Flux Fixer**

*ANSWER* Crimean War

**PAGE 20 Dan's Grand Tour**
**1** Nepal
**2** Atropos
**3** China
**4** Medderton
**5** Manchester

**PAGE 23 Flux Fixer**
*ANSWER* Liverpool

**PAGE 24 Flux Fixer**
*ANSWER* Death Zone

**PAGE 36 Flux Fixer**
*ANSWER* The Valeyard

**PAGE 38**
**1** Fact. **2** Fact. **3** Fib. **4** Fact. **5** Fib. **6** Fib. **7** Fib.

**PAGE 42 Flux Fixer**
*ANSWER* Silurians

**PAGE 44 Flux Fixer**
*ANSWER* Bad Wolf

**PAGE 46 Flux Fixer**
*ANSWER* Ravagers

**PAGE 50 Flux Fixer**
*ANSWER* Nardole

**PAGE 52 Sea-ing Double**

**B3** The ship has an extra crow's nest
**C1** Dan's belt buckle is missing
**C5** The sonic screwdriver is glowing green
**D4** The Sea Devil design is missing from the ship
**E5** The Sea Devil's sword is shorter
**E3** The Sea Devil has an extra fin

**PAGE 56 Flux Fixer**
*ANSWER* Gloucester